ALMOST TO FREEDOM

BY VAUNDA MICHEAUX NELSON
ILLUSTRATIONS BY COLIN BOOTMAN

SCHOLASTIC INC.
New York Toronto London Auckland Sydney
Mexico City New Delhi Hong Kong Buenos Aires

FOR ASHLEY
—Vaun

FOR MY BEST FRIEND, KEITH ANTHONY JONES, AND ADJUA THOMAS AND HER FAMILY. ALSO, SPECIAL THANKS TO YANEEK CAMBELL AND ANSEL PITCAIRN. THIS BOOK WOULD NOT HAVE BEEN POSSIBLE WITHOUT THEIR HELP.
—Colin

Acknowledgments: *I am especially grateful to Ashley Bryan who introduced me to the Museum of International Folk Art and gave me insight and encouragement on the manuscript. For their assistance and support, I thank: Stephanie Farrow, Lucy Hampson, Katherine Hauth, Uma Krishnaswami, Marilyn Schroeder, Lori Snyder, Jeanne W. Peterson, Jean Powell, Colin Bootman, Margaret Atwood, Ann Checchia, Ron Hussey, Bianca Spence, Phillippa Ager, Ree Mobley and the Museum of International Folk Art. Special thanks to my agent, Tracey Adams, and my editor, Ellen Stein. Finally, to my husband, Drew, for being my best editor and best friend.* —V.M.N.

The publishers have generously given permission to use an excerpt from "Five Poems for Dolls" by Margaret Atwood from the following copyrighted works: *Selected Poems II: Poems Selected and New, 1976–1986.* Copyright © 1987 by Margaret Atwood. Reprinted by permission of Houghton Mifflin Company. All rights reserved. *Selected Poems 1966–1984.* Copyright © 1990 by Margaret Atwood. Reprinted by permission of Oxford University Press Canada. *Poems 1976–1986.* Copyright © 1987 by Margaret Atwood, first published in Great Britain in 1992 by Virago Press Ltd. Reprinted in *Eating Fire: Selected Poetry 1965–1995.* Copyright © 1998 by Margaret Atwood. Reprinted by permission of Virago Press, Ltd.

ISBN 0-439-61994-7

Text copyright © 2003 by Vaunda Micheaux Nelson.
Illustrations copyright © 2003 by Colin Bootman. All rights reserved.
Published by Scholastic Inc., 557 Broadway, New York, NY 10012, by arrangement with Carolrhoda Books, Inc., a Division of Lerner Publishing Group. SCHOLASTIC and associated logos are trademarks and/or registered trademarks of Scholastic Inc.

12 11 10 9 8 7 6 5 4 3   4 5 6 7 8 9/0

Printed in the U.S.A.   24

First Scholastic printing, February 2004

A DOLL IS A WITNESS
WHO CANNOT DIE,
WITH A DOLL YOU ARE NEVER ALONE.

Margaret Atwood

I STARTED OUT no more'n a bunch of rags on a Virginia plantation. Lindy's mama was my maker. Miz Rachel done a fine job puttin' me together, takin' extra time to sew my face on real careful with thread, embroidery they call it. I don't have no hair. Miz Rachel just made a bandanna from some old cloth and tied it 'round my head like she wore. I used to think about havin' me some hair, but now it don't bother me none.

When she's done sewin', Miz Rachel give me to her little girl. Lindy hugs me hard and says, "Your name be Sally. We gonna be best friends." From that first day, when Lindy be somewheres, I be there with her.

I like how Lindy holds me at night and don't even mind when she rolls over me in her sleep. Bein' Lindy's doll baby is a right important job.

When Lindy and Miz Rachel pick cotton, I be there, too. Lindy ties me 'round her waist with a rope. The knot's kinda loose and, after a while, I fall to the ground.

"Sally, you gettin' yourself all dirty," Lindy says. "Now you stay put."

Miz Rachel wipes sweat from her brow and shows Lindy how to tie me on tight. The overseer hollers, "Git up, there!" like he's talkin' to a couple of horses. He's ridin' over carryin' his whip. Miz Rachel and Lindy quick start pickin' again.

The work be hard, but the long days seem a mite easier with everybody singin', *"Swing low, sweet chariot, comin' for to carry me home...."*

Come sundown, we sit 'round and listen to stories about little critters foolin' big ones and about slaves outsmartin' massas. These is the best times 'cause there's lotsa laughin' and singin'.

But when folks start talkin' about somethin' called Freedom, their faces turn serious in the firelight. Some say you can buy Freedom, but it's so dear we never hearda anybody ever could. Seems the only other way to get it is to run away to a place called North.

The way they talk, Freedom must be a good thing. But after
what happened to Lindy's papa, I ain't sure. Strangers chain
Mr. Henry in a wagon and take him away. "Massa sold him
down the river" is what folks say, 'cause he try to get Freedom.
Miz Rachel, she cried and cried, Lindy, too, and she hug me so
hard I think my insides'll bust out my seams.

After that, Miz Rachel sits up at night lookin' at the sky. She holds Lindy and Lindy holds me. She rocks us, singin', "*Steal away, steal away home. I ain't got long to stay here.*"

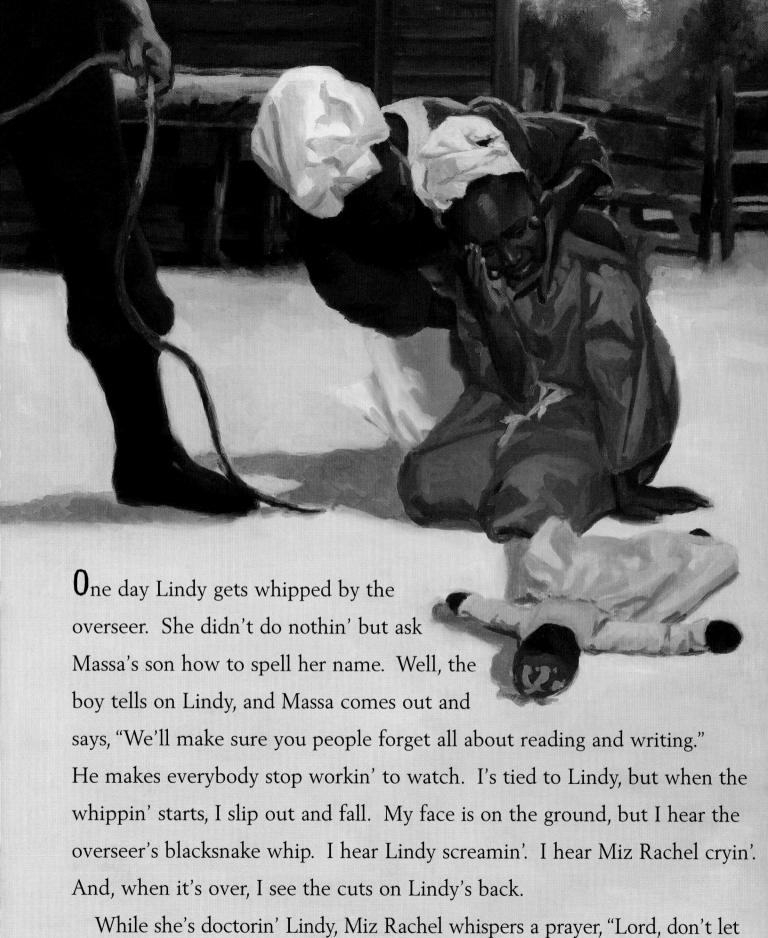

One day Lindy gets whipped by the overseer. She didn't do nothin' but ask Massa's son how to spell her name. Well, the boy tells on Lindy, and Massa comes out and says, "We'll make sure you people forget all about reading and writing." He makes everybody stop workin' to watch. I's tied to Lindy, but when the whippin' starts, I slip out and fall. My face is on the ground, but I hear the overseer's blacksnake whip. I hear Lindy screamin'. I hear Miz Rachel cryin'. And, when it's over, I see the cuts on Lindy's back.

While she's doctorin' Lindy, Miz Rachel whispers a prayer, "Lord, don't let Massa be sellin' my baby like he done her papa."

Later, Lindy sets me on a stump, her cheeks wet with tears.
"Someday, Sally, we won't be doin' what Massa say. We be
goin' to Freedom."

I'm thinkin', "Lord, have mercy!"

One night, Lindy's sleepin' beside me like always. Then there's whisperin', and Lindy's gettin' her clothes on. The sun ain't awake yet, but field workers is always up 'fore dawn, so I don't think much of it. Miz Rachel's all dressed and tellin' Lindy, "Hurry now, but hush." Lindy grabs me up and ties me to her. The way Lindy's heart's beatin' I know somethin' important's happenin'.

Lindy takes Miz Rachel's hand, and we sneak
out behind our shack and run into the night. I know
I ain't runnin', but it feels like I am. Feels like I'm flyin'.
Branches slap us along the way like they scoldin',
warnin' us to go back. But Miz Rachel don't pay no mind.
Just keeps runnin'.

"My feet, Mama. There's burs," Lindy says.
"I know, Baby," Miz Rachel whispers. "But we gotta keep on."
We run for a while, then hide under the brush,
then we run some more. Lindy's breathin' hard,
but says, "Don't be worryin', Sally. Mama
say we be with Papa soon." Soon don't
come *real* soon.

But, sure enough, Mr. Henry's waitin' by the river. He hugs Miz Rachel. Then he lifts Lindy into the air and me with her.

"Papa!" Lindy says laughin', but Mr. Henry covers her mouth and holds her close.

"Quiet, now! We gotta get to the boatman and cross over."

We hurry along the bank to where the man is waitin' with his skiff. Without one word, we climb in. The night is dark as inside a possum. It's dead quiet 'cept for the sound of the boatman pushin', pushin', pushin' his oars. My face soaks up little splashes of water as we glide along.

On the other side, Miz Rachel squeezes the boatman's hand. Lindy's papa leads us through the night woods.

We run and hide, run and hide, 'til we come to a house with a lantern glowin' soft in the window. We crouch behind the barn. Lindy's papa calls out —"Whoo! Whoo!"—like a hooty owl. The lantern goes out.

A white man wearin' eyeglasses steps out of the dark. He motions us to follow him to the back of the house.

Inside the kitchen, a woman with silver hair opens a door to a storeroom. The man lifts a rug, takes some boards from the floor, and uncovers a ladder leadin' into pitch darkness.

"It's small and a mite chilly," the man says, "but it's the safest place we've got." He hands Miz Rachel a lantern.

"I've put blankets and water down there, and I'll get you some food," the woman says.

"Much obliged, ma'am," Mr. Henry says, and he climbs down the ladder.

The woman hands Lindy a pillow. Miz Rachel's friend who worked in the big house told us about pillows, but I never seen one.

The secret room is tiny, but not much smaller than the shack Massa had us in. Miz Rachel spreads two blankets on the dirt floor, and everybody 'cept me takes some water. Lindy lays me on the pillow. It's the softest thing. Like a cloud from heaven.

The silver-haired woman hands down a stew pot, bowls, some bread, and cheese. Then she closes up the floor. Miz Rachel serves up supper. Nobody talks. Too tired. Too scared. They sop up the last of their stew with bread.

"Sleep now," Papa says to Lindy and me.

Lindy whispers she needs to make water. Mr. Henry points to a bucket in the corner. "Privy be too dangerous."

After, Lindy holds me close like always. She lays her head on that pillow and smiles. "'Night, Sally," she whispers. "We almost to Freedom."

If I coulda, I'da smiled, too.

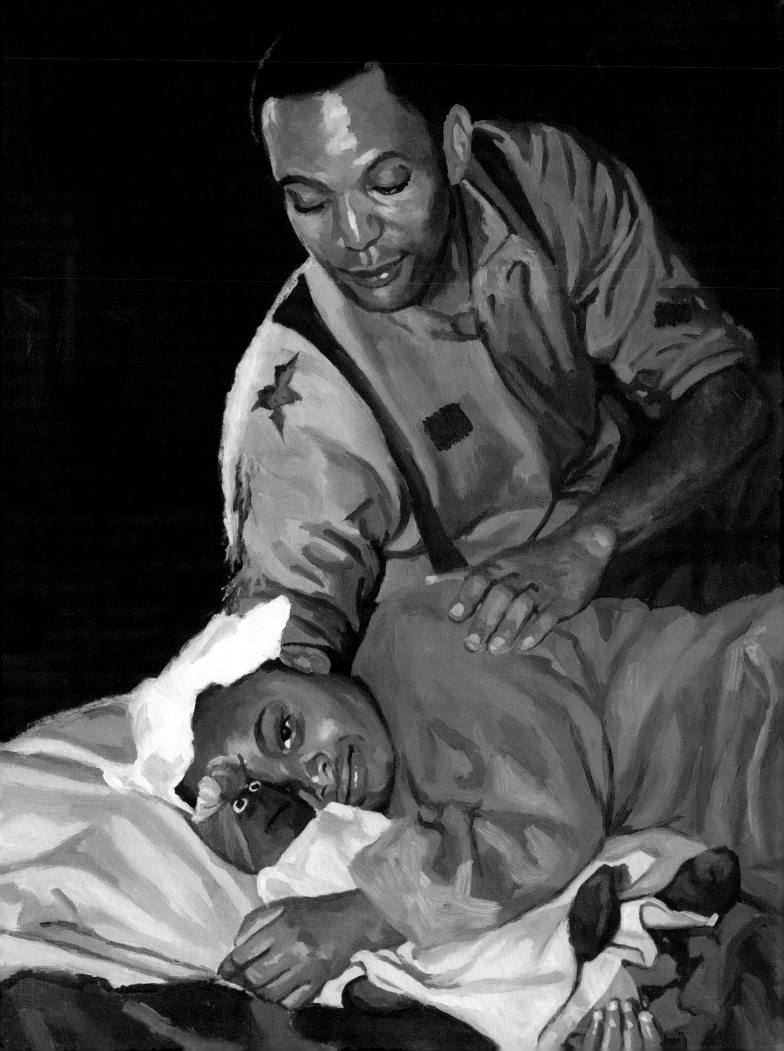

Seems like we just get to sleep and Miz Rachel is shakin'
Lindy, "Come on, Baby. Quick!"
   "Why?" Lindy asks.
   "Slave catchers," Mr. Henry whispers, blowin' out the lantern.

Lindy ties me 'round her waist. I guess sleep still has her 'cause the knot ain't tight. Miz Rachel tucks some bread and cheese in her apron, and she and Lindy follow Mr. Henry up the ladder. They're scramblin' fast, and I feel myself slippin'. Then I'm fallin', fallin' till I hit that dirt floor. Lindy calls my name. The silver-haired woman is closin' up the floor. *Lindy! Wait!* But she can't hear me, 'cause I ain't got no voice. The boards shut out the light.

When the floorboards open again, sunlight shines in. The silver-haired woman comes down the ladder.

"*There* you are," she says, pickin' me up. "Your little mama didn't want to leave you." She straightens my dress. "There just wasn't time." She sets me on a blanket and tucks it 'round me. "Sleep tight," she says, and carries the lantern and privy bucket up the ladder. Then she closes the floor.

If I coulda made tears, them blankets woulda been wet clean through. I want Lindy. But I know she ain't comin' back. Can't. The loneliness swallows me up.

I give a lot of time to thinkin' about Lindy and her folks, where they was, and if they ever got to Freedom like they was wantin'. I give a lot of time to prayin' they did. And I give a lot of time to grievin'. Grievin' for myself. I wish the silver-haired woman would come. But she don't. Nobody comes.

After a spell, I'm thinkin' maybe slave catchers is watchin' this house. Maybe the hidin' place ain't safe. Maybe I'll lay right here for the rest of my days.

By and by, a mouse scurries over my face and into a corner.
I's glad to have the company. I pass the time listenin' to
Miz Mouse make herself a nest and raise her young'uns.
I's sorry when they finally go 'cause I get to feelin' lonely
again. I get to thinkin' that I best stop hopin'.

Then one day, praise the Lord, the boards bein' moved!
Somebody's comin' down the ladder! If I'd a flesh-and-
blood heart, it woulda been poundin' like Lindy's that night
we run off.

I see light from a lantern and a woman wrappin' up a
little girl in a blanket. The child's shiverin', more scared,
I think, than cold. Her eyes look tired and tearful.

The woman picks me up and says, "Willa, darlin', this must be the
dolly the missus was mentionin'." She blows the dust off my face
and holds me closer to the lantern. "Mighty fine stitchin'."
"Can I keep her?" the girl asks. Her mama nods, and Willa
hugs me so hard I think
my insides'll bust
out my seams.

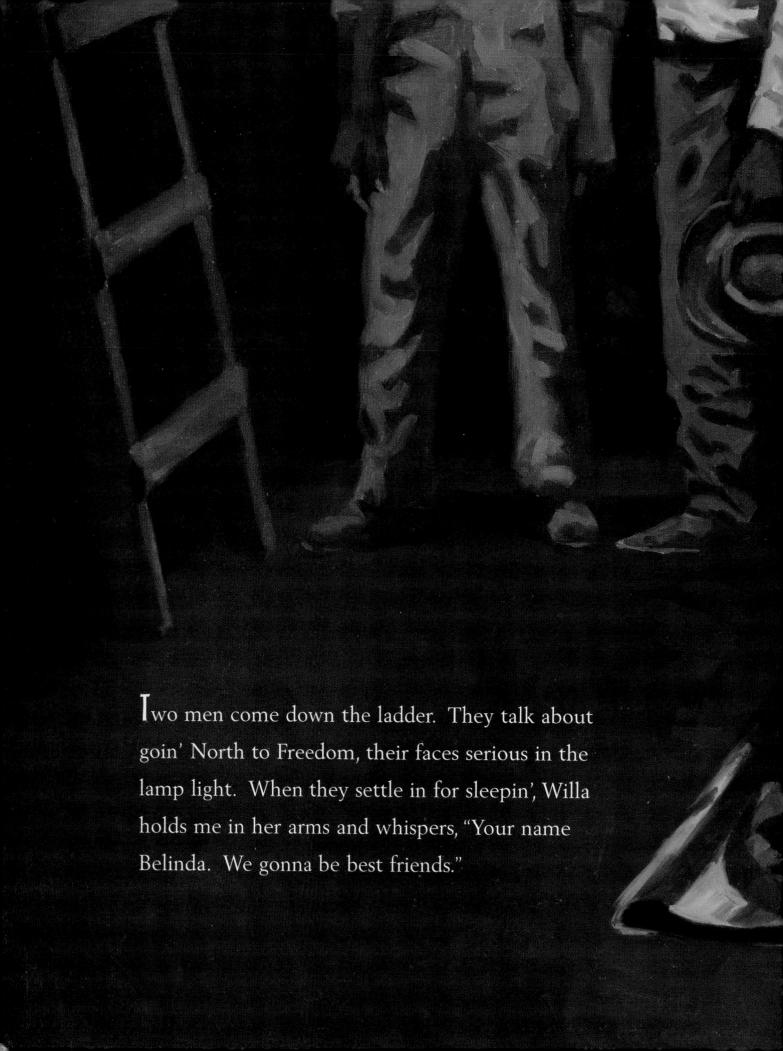

Two men come down the ladder. They talk about goin' North to Freedom, their faces serious in the lamp light. When they settle in for sleepin', Willa holds me in her arms and whispers, "Your name Belinda. We gonna be best friends."

Belinda. I like that. Sounds like Lindy. My face don't change, but I smiles inside, rememberin' the cracklin' of the straw mattress when Lindy'd roll over me in her sleep. I sure do miss her, but I's mighty glad to be Willa's doll baby. It's a right important job.

AUTHOR'S NOTE

I WAS INSPIRED to write *Almost to Freedom* during a visit to the Museum of International Folk Art in Santa Fe, New Mexico. There, a display of black rag dolls from the 1800s and 1900s immediately caught my attention. "The majority of the dolls were entirely handmade from scrap cloth," my husband read from the museum guidebook. "A few were said to have been found in one of the hideouts of the Underground Railroad, suggesting their use by black children." As I admired the exhibit, my husband leaned in close and whispered, "There's a story in that." *Yes*, I thought, *if only those dolls could talk.*

The Girard Collection, Case 8-12, Multiple Visions Exhibition, The Museum of International Folk Art (a unit of the Museum of New Mexico, Santa Fe)

The Underground Railroad was most active between 1830 and the beginning of the Civil War in 1861. This was not a real railroad with trains that traveled beneath the earth. It was a secret network of courageous people, black and white, who worked together to help slaves steal away to freedom in northern and western states and to Canada. No one person knew the entire system of escape routes and safe houses, and some details remain unknown to this day.

Dedicated individuals like the boatman, the silver-haired woman, and her husband, risked much to be part of this movement. Runaways faced even greater dangers. Although some were transported by ship, wagon, or train, most traveled on foot through woods, swamps, fields, and rivers, often pursued by slave catchers with dogs. Some slaves reached freedom. Others were caught, returned to their masters, and punished severely. Many captured runaways were whipped savagely or

sold, never to see their families again. Some were fitted with iron collars, painfully shackled, or had their toes cut off to keep them from running away again. Still, thousands of slaves escaped through the Underground Railroad.

HISTORICAL WORDS AND PHRASES

big house: the slave owner's home

dear: expensive

make water: urinate

massa: a slaveholder usually expected his slaves to call him "master." *Massa* was a deliberate misuse or corruption of the term, used by slaves to diminish the respect "master" commands.

overseer: a person who directed or supervised the work of slaves; sometimes called a "slave driver" because of the harsh treatment he inflicted

privy: an outhouse

skiff: a small, flat-bottomed boat

slave catchers: white men paid by slave owners to track and capture runaway slaves within and beyond the local area. Patrollers or "paddyrollers" were another threat to escaping slaves. Patrollers were hired by communities to police the plantation countryside.

Steal away . . . : an example of a slave song. While songs provided comfort and entertainment, many were sung to pass along messages about secret meetings and escape plans.